Mustard & Pepper

Written by
Alasdair Hutton

Illustrated by
William Gorman

Curlytale
Books

Mustard and Pepper lived in a big family with lots of children and lots of other dogs in a lovely house with large gardens.

The house was Abbotsford, the Borders home of the famous writer Sir Walter Scott. He had four children and Mustard and Pepper were his Dandie Dinmont terriers.

Mustard and Pepper loved chasing things. But because they had quite short legs, they didn't often catch them!

One day the children, Sophia, Walter, Anne and Charles went to play hide and seek in the woods with Mustard and Pepper, Finette the setter and Hamlet the young greyhound.

2

Walter always wanted to start so he covered his eyes and began to count.

"...97, 98, 99, 100! Coming ready or not!"

All the dogs rushed to a holly bush, barking, so Walter found Sophia very easily.

Mustard and Pepper jumped all over Charles who was hiding behind a low wall, so he was found quickly too. "Daft dogs!" he said, laughing.

"But where's Anne?" Walter looked around.
She wasn't in any of her usual hiding spots.

"Shhh!" said Sophia. "I can hear somebody crying.
It must be Anne."

The dogs dashed off after the sound, closely followed by the children and soon found Anne.

Walter comforted his little sister. "You're not lost," he said. "We've found you."

"I know I'm not lost," said Anne. "But my necklace is."

Anne's necklace was her pride and joy. Her father had brought it back from Edinburgh as a present for her eighth birthday.

"Don't worry," said Charles. "Greyhounds are very good at spotting things, especially something which shines. Hamlet will find it. Come on boy!"

And off they went along the path by the river, looking this way and that.

Mustard and Pepper and Walter and Anne and Sophia and Finette waited...and waited...

High overhead they could hear the birds calling in the trees including the harsh screech of the magpies.

But Charles and Hamlet returned with glum faces... and without the necklace.

"Sorry Anne," said Charles.

Mustard and Pepper rushed around looking very enthusiastic. Was it their turn to try and find Anne's necklace?

"Woof!" barked Mustard.

"Woof woof!" barked Pepper.

But it still wasn't their turn.

8

"Please don't cry, Anne," said Sophia kindly. "Finette will sniff out your necklace. Setters are excellent sniffers. Come on!"

And Sophia and Finette disappeared.

Mustard and Pepper and Walter and Anne and Charles and Hamlet waited... and waited...

But Sophia and Finette returned with glum faces. "Sorry, Anne," said Sophia. "We went round in circles. But we didn't find your necklace."

Mustard and Pepper rushed around looking very eager. Surely it was their turn to try and find Anne's favourite necklace?

"Woof!" barked Mustard.
"Woof Woof!" barked Pepper.

But the children paid no attention.

Walter, Sophia and Charles looked worried, and Anne started to cry again.

"Woof!" barked Mustard.

"Woof Woof!" barked Pepper.

They rushed around more enthusiastically and more eagerly than ever.

"Settle down, lads," said Walter. "We have to find Anne's necklace, not chase it."

He rubbed their ears, but he didn't ask them to help.

"I think we should search at home," said Walter.
The bigger dogs ran ahead towards the house.
But Mustard and Pepper only had short legs. By
the time they got home the other dogs were already
busy searching.

"Woof!" barked Mustard.

"Woof Woof!" barked Pepper.

"Shhh!" said Walter. "We're searching, not barking."

There was a lot of sniffing and wagging of tails as Hamlet and Finette poked under tables and sniffed behind chairs.

Even Maida, Papa's great big deer hound, joined in. But he was a bit too big.

Bang, crash, wallop!

He knocked over a suit of armour.
It was one of Papa's favourite treasures.
So Maida went for a lie down.

There was still no sign of Anne's necklace.

16

Mustard and Pepper tried to cheer the children up by running in circles and jumping and twisting. That usually made everybody laugh.

But not today.

"Settle down, lads."

Walter, Sophia and Charles looked terribly glum.

Anne was still crying.

There was a chittering in the garden. A red squirrel was running around searching for any stray nuts which might have been dropped there.

Mustard looked at Pepper and Pepper looked at Mustard. They couldn't help themselves. Here was something they could do so they dashed out of the front door and chased the red squirrel.

Down the lawn, along the river, into the woods.
They chased him past the oak tree.
They chased him past the elm tree.

But when he reached the Scots Pine tree the red squirrel ran all the way to the top.

"Woof!" barked Mustard.

"Woof Woof!" barked Pepper.

The two dogs could not follow so they ran round and round the tree trunk until they were dizzy.

All of a sudden from the top of the tree they heard a lot of excited chittering and a lot of angry screeching.

Off flew the thieving magpie – furious to lose the beautiful prize that he had found.

Down scampered the red squirrel and 'thump' - something shiny landed on the ground.

Triumphantly Mustard took the necklace in his mouth. Pepper chased Mustard all the way back to the house.

"Woof Woof!" barked Pepper.
Mustard's mouth was too full to bark. He dropped the necklace into Anne's lap.

"Oh thank you!" said Anne, and she stopped crying and gave both the dogs a huge hug. Walter ruffled their ears.
"Well done, lads," he said. "You deserve a treat."
As they waited after supper for Papa to tell them a story, Sophia, Walter, Anne and Charles all agreed that they would play hide and seek again the next day.

"But I don't think I'll wear my necklace," said Anne.

Mustard and Pepper curled up by the fire and slept, and slept and slept.

24

About the Author & Illustrator

Alasdair Hutton has been the voice of the Royal Edinburgh Milita Tattoo for twenty-eight years entertaining audiences from all over the world on the Esplanade of Edinburgh Castle every summer.

He has worked as a journalist in Australia and Scotland and as a broadcaster with the BBC. He represented the South of Scotland the European Parliament for ten years and was a local councillor the Borders for another decade, including nine as the Convener Council.

Alasdair served for twenty-two years as a volunteer paratrooper i the Scottish Battalion of the famous Parachute Regiment and no raises funds for charities helping military veterans.

He has written five books before Mustard and Pepper, three for children and two for adults. He would like to dedicate this book t Mortimer Hutton.

William Gorman is a graduate of Duncan of Jordanstone College of Art and Design in Dundee where he studied Illustration and Print-making.
After travelling in New Zealand for a year he returned to his native Galloway where he worked for an archive newspaper company before setting up in business as an artist.

He lives and works in Wigtown, Scotland's National Booktown.

This is his first book for children.

ISBN: 978-1-9996336-1-5
Published by Curly Tale Books Ltd
34 Main Street
Kirkcowan DG8 0HG
www.curlytalebooks.co.uk
Printed by J&B Print, 32A Albert Street, Newton Stewart, DG8 6EJ

The great storyteller and writer Sir Walter Scott built a grand house for his family around an old farmhouse beside the River Tweed in the Scottish Borders. He called it Abbotsford. You can visit it today to see where the family lived and played.

Sir Walter Scott and his wife Charlotte had four children - Sophia, Walter, Anne and Charles. Sir Walter Scott loved dogs and there were always plenty of them in the household.

In Guy Mannering, a famous novel written by Sir Walter Scott, there is a character called Dandie Dinmont, a cheerful farmer who had a lot of terriers, called either Mustard or Pepper. Sir Walter Scott's books were bestsellers - he was as popular then as JK Rowling is now - and a breed of terriers with a long body, short legs and a tuft of hair on the top of their heads came to be named after Dandie Dinmont and were great favourites of Sir Walter.

If you visit the Scott Monument in Princes Street Gardens in Edinburgh you will see beside his statue a stone sculpture of Maida, Sir Walter's beloved hound. In this story you also met Hamlet, the young, boisterous, black greyhound who had to be kept in order by Maida, and Finette - a beautiful setter with silken hair, long pendent ears and a mild eye who belonged to Lady Scott.

Printed in the UK
on 100% recycled paper

The challenges our planet faces as a result of human activity are many - and we at Curly Tale Books believe that every action can make a difference. We are proud to have been awarded the GSA Biosphere Certification Mark which means that:
-we operate in a way that minimises our impact on the environment
-we look after and promote our Biosphere, educating others about why it is special
-we work together with local people and businesses, using and promoting their products
-we actively support our local community

Other Titles From Curly Tale Books
www.curlytalebooks.co.uk

Big Bill the Beltie Bull

Written & illustrated

Big Bill's Beltie Bairns

written by
Jayne Baldwin
illustrated by
Shalla Gray

Nip Nebs

Susi Briggs & Ruthie Redden

Charlotte's Woolly Yarn
A Spin Around South-West Scotland

Written & Illustrated
by
Shalla Gray

Big Bill and the Larking Lambs

Written by
Jayne Baldwin
Illustrated by
Shalla Gray